Your Favourite
THOMAS THE TANK ENGINE
Story Collection

DEAN

Contents

Thomas in Trouble

There is a line to a quarry at the end of Thomas's branch line. It goes for some distance along by the road. Thomas was always very careful there in case anyone was coming. "Peep, pip, peep!" he whistled, then people got out of the way and he puffed slowly along, with his trucks rumbling behind him.

Early one morning there was a policeman standing close to the line. Thomas liked policemen. He had been a great friend of the Constable who used to live in the village.

"Peep, peep! Good morning!" Thomas whistled.

Thomas expected that this new policeman would be as friendly as the other one. He was sorry to see that the policeman didn't look friendly at all.

The policeman was red in the face and very cross. "Disgraceful!" he spluttered. "I didn't sleep a wink last night – it was *so* quiet." The policeman looked at Thomas. "And now," he said, "engines come whistling suddenly behind me!"

"I'm sorry, sir," said Thomas. "I only said 'good morning' to you."

"Where is your cow-catcher?" he asked, sharply.

"But, I don't catch cows, sir," said Thomas.

"Don't be funny!" snapped the policeman. He looked at Thomas's wheels. "No side plates, either!" he muttered and he wrote in his notebook.

Then he spoke sternly to Thomas. "Engines going on public roads must have their wheels covered and a cow-catcher in front. You haven't so *you* are dangerous to the public."

"Rubbish!" said Thomas's driver. "We've been along here hundreds of times and there has never been an accident."

"That makes it worse," said the policeman. And he wrote "REGULAR LAW BREAKER" in his book.

Thomas's driver climbed back into the cab and Thomas puffed sadly away.

7

The Fat Controller was having breakfast. He was eating toast and marmalade. His wife had just given him some more coffee.

The butler came in.

"Excuse me, sir," he said. "You are wanted on the telephone."

"Bother that telephone!" said the Fat Controller.

"I am sorry, my dear," he said a few minutes later. "Thomas is in trouble with the police and I must go at once." He gulped down his coffee and hurried from the room.

At the station, Thomas's driver told the Fat Controller what had happened.

"Dangerous to the public indeed! We'll see about that!" said the Fat Controller.

The policeman came onto the platform and the Fat Controller spoke to him at once. But however much the Fat Controller argued with him . . . it was no good.

"The law is the law," said the policeman, "and we can't change it."

The Fat Controller felt quite exhausted. "I'm sorry," he said to Thomas's driver. "It's no use arguing with policemen. We will have to make those cow-catcher things for Thomas, I suppose."

"Everyone will laugh, sir," said Thomas, sadly. "They will say that I look like a tram."

The Fat Controller stared at Thomas and then he laughed. "Well done, Thomas! Why didn't I think of it before?" he said. "We want a tram engine," he went on. "When I was on my holiday, I met a nice little engine called Toby. He hasn't enough work to do and he needs a change. I'll write to his Controller at once!"

A few days later Toby arrived.

"That's a good engine," said the Fat Controller. "I see that you have brought Henrietta with you."

"You don't mind, do you, sir?" asked Toby, anxiously. "The Station Master wanted to use her as a hen house, and that would never do."

"No, indeed," said the Fat Controller, gravely. "We couldn't allow that!"

Toby made the trucks behave even better than Thomas did. At first, Thomas was jealous, but he was so pleased when Toby rang his bell and made the policeman jump that they have been firm friends ever since.

Percy Runs Away

When Thomas the Tank Engine was given his own branch line there was only Edward who would do the shunting for the big engines. Edward liked shunting and playing with trucks, but the others would not help him. They said that shunting was not a job for important Tender Engines, it was a job for common Tank Engines.

The Fat Controller was very cross. He kept them in the shed and said that they could only come out when they stopped being naughty. Then he sent for Thomas to come and help Edward to run the line for a few days.

Henry, James and Gordon were in the shed for several days. They were very miserable and longed to be let out. At last, the Fat Controller arrived.

"I hope that you are sorry," he said sternly, "and understand that you are not so important after all." He told them that he had a surprise for them!

"We have a new Tank Engine called Percy. He is a smart little green engine, with four wheels. Percy has helped to pull the coaches and Thomas and Edward have worked the main line very nicely, while you have been away."

"But I will let you out now if you promise to be good," he said.

"Yes, sir," said the three engines. "We will."

"That's right," said the Fat Controller. "But please remember that this 'no shunting' nonsense must stop."

The Fat Controller told Thomas, Edward and Percy that they could go and play on the branch line for a few days. They ran off happily to find Annie and Clarabel at the junction. Annie and Clarabel were Thomas's two coaches and they were very pleased to see Thomas back again. Edward and Percy played with the trucks.

"Stop! Stop! Stop!" screamed the trucks as they were pushed into their proper sidings. But the two engines laughed and went on shunting until the trucks were in their right places.

Next, Edward took some trucks to the Quarry.

Percy was left alone, but he didn't mind a bit. He liked watching the trains and being cheeky to the other engines.

"Hurry, hurry, hurry," he would call and they got very cross.

After a great deal of shunting on Thomas's branch line, Percy was waiting for the signalman to set the points so that he could get back to the yard. He was eager to work, but he was being rather careless and was not paying attention.

Edward had told Percy about the signals on the main line.

"Be careful on that main line," he warned. "Whistle to the signalman to let him know that you are there."

But Percy forgot all about Edward's warning. He didn't remember to whistle and the signalman forgot he was there. Percy waited and waited. The points were still against him so he couldn't move. Then he looked along the main line.

"Peep! Peep!" he whistled in horror. "Peep! peep!" he whistled again, for rushing straight towards him was Gordon with the Express.

Percy's driver turned on full steam and shouted for Percy to go back. But Percy's wheels wouldn't turn quickly enough and Gordon couldn't stop.

Percy waited for the crash. The driver and fireman jumped out.

"Oo . . . ooh!" groaned Gordon. "Get out of my way!"

Percy opened his eyes. Gordon had stopped with Percy's buffers just a few inches from his own. But Percy had begun to move.

"I won't stay here. I'll run away!" he puffed.

He went straight through Edward's station and was so frightened that he ran right up Gordon's hill without stopping. After that he was tired, but he couldn't stop. Percy had no driver to shut off steam and put on his brakes.

"I shall have to run till my wheels wear out!" panted Percy. "Oh dear! Oh dear! I want to stop! I want to stop!" he puffed.

The man in the signal box saw that Percy was in trouble, so he kindly set the points.

Percy puffed wearily into a nice empty siding. He was too tired now to care where he went.

"I – want – to – stop! I – want – to – stop!" he puffed.

"I have stopped! I have stopped!" he said, thankfully. "Sssh . . . Sssh!" he gasped as he ended up in a big bank of earth.

"Never mind, Percy," said the workmen as they dug him out. "You shall have a drink and some coal and then you'll feel better."

Gordon had arrived.

"Well done, Percy! You started so quickly that you stopped a nasty accident!"

"I'm sorry I was cheeky," said Percy. "You were clever to stop."

Then Gordon helped to pull Percy out from the bank. Now Percy helps with the coaches in the yard. He is still cheeky because he is that sort of engine, but he is always *very* careful when he goes on the main line.

Thomas and the Breakdown Train

Every day the Fat Controller came to the station to catch his train. He always walked over to have a word with Thomas the Tank Engine.

"Hello, Thomas," he said. "Remember to be patient. You can never be as strong and fast as Gordon, the big blue engine, but you can be a Really Useful Engine. Don't let those trucks tease you."

There were lots of trucks at the station. They were silly and noisy. They talked too much and played tricks on engines that they were not used to. Thomas worked very hard, pushing and pulling the trucks into place and getting them ready for the big engines to take on long journeys. There was also a small coach and two strange things that his driver called *cranes*.

"That's the breakdown train," he told Thomas. "The cranes are for lifting heavy things like engines and coaches and trucks."

One day, Thomas was very busy in the yard. Suddenly, he heard an engine whistling, "Help! Help!" When he looked towards the line he saw a goods train come rushing through, much too fast.

Thomas could see that it was James – and James looked very frightened. He was screaming and whistling. His brake blocks were on fire!

"They're pushing me! They're pushing me!" he panted.

But the trucks were laughing. They were having lots of fun with James. Poor James went faster and faster. He was still whistling and calling for help as he disappeared down the line.

"I'd like to teach those trucks a lesson," said Thomas.

Then came the alarm.

"James is off the line! Fetch the breakdown train – quickly!" shouted one of the men.

Thomas was coupled on to the breakdown train and off they went. Thomas worked his hardest.

"Hurry! Hurry! Hurry!" he puffed.

"Bother those trucks and their tricks. I hope poor James isn't hurt," said Thomas as he hurried along.

They found James at a bend in the line. He was in a field with a cow looking at him.

James's driver and the fireman were feeling him all over to see if he was hurt.

"Never mind, James," they said. "It wasn't your fault. It was those wooden brakes they gave you. We always said they were no good."

Thomas pushed the breakdown train alongside James. Then he pulled the unhurt trucks out of the way.

"Oh dear! Oh dear!" they groaned.

"Serves you right. Serves you right," puffed Thomas. He was hard at work puffing backwards and forwards all afternoon.

"This'll teach you a lesson. This'll teach you a lesson," he told the trucks.

They left the broken trucks and then, with two cranes, they put James back on the rails. He tried to move, but he couldn't. So Thomas helped him back to the shed.

The Fat Controller was waiting anxiously for them. He smiled when he saw Thomas.

"Well, Thomas," he said. "I've heard all about it, and I'm very pleased with you. You are a Really Useful Engine!"

"James shall have some proper brakes and a new coat of paint," he said. "And Thomas, you shall have a branch line all to yourself!"

"Oh! Thank you, sir!" said Thomas, feeling very proud.

Now Thomas is as happy as can be. He has a branch line and two coaches called Annie and Clarabel. Annie can only take passengers and Clarabel can take passengers, luggage and a guard.

They are both old and need new paint, but Thomas puffs proudly backwards and forwards with them, all day.

He is never lonely. His friends, Edward and Henry, stop quite often to tell him the news.

Gordon, the biggest and proudest engine, is always in a hurry, but he never forgets to say, "Poop, poop," and Thomas always whistles, "Peep, peep," in return.

Edward, Gordon and Henry

Gordon, the Big Engine, always pulls the express. He is very proud of being the only engine strong enough to do so. One day Gordon left the station with the express as usual. It was full of important people, like the Fat Controller, and Gordon was seeing just how fast he could go.

"Hurry! Hurry!" he said.

"Trickety-trock, trickety-trock, trickety-trock," said the coaches.

Gordon went very fast and soon he could see the tunnel where Henry stood, bricked up and lonely.

Henry had been very foolish. He had gone into the tunnel and wouldn't come out again because he was afraid that the rain would spoil his lovely green paint.

The guard had blown his whistle; the fireman and passengers had argued with him; the men had pulled and pushed him but still Henry would not move. Then, at last, they had given up. The Fat Controller had ordered the men to take up the old rails and to build a wall in front of Henry. The other engines had to use the tunnel at the other side. Now Henry wondered if he would ever pull trains again.

"Oh dear! Will the Fat Controller ever forgive me and let me out?" he said to himself that day, as he watched Gordon getting closer and closer to the tunnel.

"In a minute," Gordon said, "I'm going to poop-poop at Henry and rush through the tunnel and out again into the open!"

He was almost there when, crack, "WHEE———EESHSH!"

And suddenly, there he was, going slower and slower in a cloud of steam. His driver stopped the train.

"What has happened to me?" asked Gordon. "I feel so weak."

"You've burst a safety valve," said the driver. "You can't pull the train any more."

"Oh dear," said Gordon. "We were going so nicely, too. And look, there's Henry laughing at me!"

All the passengers climbed out of the coaches and came to see Gordon.

"Humph!" said the Fat Controller. "I never liked these big engines – always going wrong. Send for another engine at once."

They uncoupled Gordon. He had just enough puff to slink slowly into the siding, out of the way.

The guard went back to the yard to fetch another engine. There was only Edward left in the shed.

"Gordon has burst a safety valve. Can you help?" asked the guard.

"I'll come and try," said Edward.

When Edward and the guard arrived back at the tunnel, Gordon was very rude. "Pooh!" he said. "Edward can't pull the train."

But they took no notice and Edward was coupled up behind the express. Edward puffed and pushed and pushed and puffed, but he couldn't move the heavy coaches.

"I told you so," said Gordon, rudely. "Why not let Henry try?"

"Yes, I will," said the Fat Controller. "Henry, will you help to pull this train?" he asked.

"Oh yes!" said Henry, at once. "At last," he said to himself, "the Fat Controller *has* forgiven me."

So Gordon's driver and fireman lit Henry's fire. They broke down the wall and put back the rails. When Henry had built up steam, he puffed backwards out of the tunnel.

He was dirty and his boiler was black. He was covered in cobwebs. "Ooh! I'm so stiff. I'm so stiff," he groaned.

"Have a run to ease your joints and then find a turntable," said the Fat Controller, kindly.

When Henry came back he felt much better. Then they coupled him up at the front of Gordon's coaches.

"Peep, peep!" said Edward. "I'm ready!"

"Peep, peep, peep!" said Henry. "So am I!"

They started off. "Pull hard. We'll do it. Push hard. We'll do it," they puffed together.

Slowly the heavy coaches jerked and began to move. Then off they went, leaving Gordon alone in the siding. They went faster and faster. "We've done it together! We've done it together!" said Edward and Henry.

"You've done it, hurray! You've done it, hurray!" sang the coaches.

All the passengers were excited. The Fat Controller leaned out of the window to wave to Henry and Edward. But the train was going so fast that his hat blew off into a field where a goat ate it for tea!

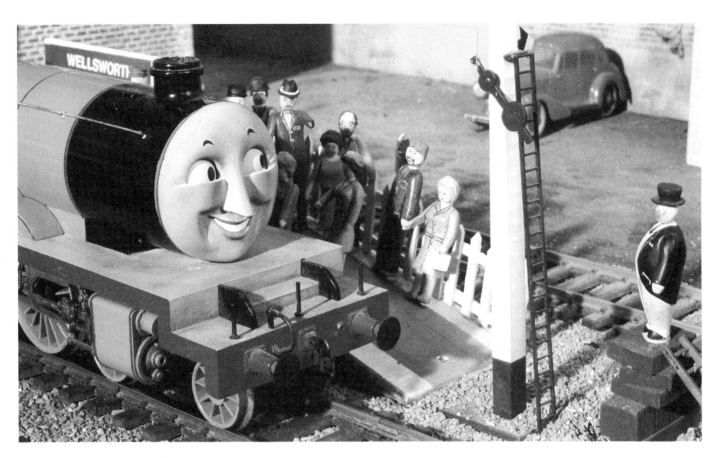

The engines didn't stop until they came to the station at the end of the line. All the passengers climbed out and thanked Henry and Edward. The Fat Controller was very pleased. He promised Henry a new coat of paint. On their way home, Edward and Henry helped Gordon back to the shed.

All three engines are now great friends. Henry doesn't mind the rain any more. He knows that the best way to keep his paint looking nice is not to run into tunnels but to ask his driver to rub him down when the day's work is over.

Thomas Goes Fishing

Thomas the Tank Engine had his own branch line. It was his reward for helping James, the Red Engine. The trucks had pushed James off the rails and Thomas had helped to rescue him. Thomas was very proud of his branch line. Every day he puffed up and down with his two coaches, Annie and Clarabel. He always looked forward to something special . . . the river.

As he rumbled over the bridge he would see people fishing down below. He often wanted to stay and watch. But his driver always said, "No! What would the Fat Controller say if we were late?"

Thomas still thought it would be lovely to stop by the river and do some fishing. Every time Thomas met another engine, he would say, "I want to fish." But they all gave the same answer, "Engines don't go fishing!"

And that's just what James said as he passed Thomas that day.

One day, Thomas stopped as usual to take in water at the station by the river. Then he saw a big painted notice. It read, "OUT OF ORDER". Thomas was very thirsty. The driver had an idea. They could get water from the river!

They found a bucket and some rope and went to the bridge. Then the driver let the bucket down into the water. The bucket was old and had five holes. So they had to fill it, pull it up, and empty it into Thomas's tank as quickly as they could, again and again. At last they were finished.

"That's good! That's good!" puffed Thomas, as he started off again, with Annie and Clarabel running happily behind.

They puffed along the valley until suddenly, Thomas began to feel a pain in his boiler. Steam began to hiss from his safety valve in an alarming way.

"There's too much steam," said his driver. The fireman tried to let more water into the boiler, but none came.

"Oh dear!" groaned Thomas. "I'm going to burst! I'm going to burst!"

They damped down his fire and he struggled on.

"I've got such a pain! I've got such a pain!" Thomas hissed.

They stopped outside the last station and Annie and Clarabel were uncoupled. The driver ran Thomas onto a siding, right out of the way.

He was still hissing, fit to burst. Then the guard telephoned for an Engine Inspector and the driver found two notices. They were written in large letters and read, "DANGER. KEEP AWAY".

Soon the Inspector and the Fat Controller arrived.

"Cheer up, Thomas!" they said. "We'll soon put you right."

The driver told them what had happened. The Engine Inspector thought that the trouble must be in the feed pipe. The Inspector climbed up to have a look. He peered in and then came down.

"Excuse me, sir," he said. "Please look in the tank and tell me what you see."

So the Fat Controller clambered up, looked in and nearly fell off in surprise!

31

"Inspector," he whispered, "can you see *fish*?"

"Gracious, goodness me! How did the fish get there, Driver?" asked the Inspector.

"We must have fished them out of the river with our bucket!" said Thomas's driver.

"Well, Thomas. So you and your driver have been fishing. But fish don't suit you. We must get them out," said the Fat Controller.

They took turns at fishing in Thomas's tank. The Fat Controller looked on and told them how to do it. When they had caught all the fish, they had a lovely picnic supper of fish and chips.

"That was good!" said the Fat Controller, as he finished off his share. "But fish don't suit *you*, Thomas. So you mustn't do it again."

"No, sir, I won't," said Thomas sadly. "Engines don't go fishing. It's too uncomfortable!"

James and the Troublesome Trucks

James had not seen the Fat Controller for some time. Not since the day when he had nearly lost his red coat and had been painted blue instead. That was the time when James had been very naughty. First he had let off steam and sprayed water on the Fat Controller's new top-hat. Then he had run too fast and made a hole in one of the coaches. The driver had had to mend the hole with newspaper and a passenger's bootlace.

The Fat Controller had been very angry. Now James was alone in the shed. He was not even allowed out to push coaches and trucks in the yard.

At last the Fat Controller arrived and came to see him.

"I can see that you are sorry, James," he said. "I hope now that you will be a better engine. You have given me a lot of trouble," said the Fat Controller. "People are laughing at my railway, and I do not like it at all."

James said that he was very sorry and promised to be a better engine.

The Fat Controller said, "I want you to pull some trucks for me."

James was delighted and puffed away.

"Here are your trucks, James," said Thomas the Tank Engine. "Have you got some bootlaces ready?" Thomas ran off, laughing.

"Oh! Oh! Oh!" said the trucks. "We want a proper engine, not a red monster."

But James took no notice and started as soon as the guard was ready.

"Come along, come along," he puffed. But the trucks were being naughty.

"We won't! We won't!" they screamed.

James took no notice and he pulled the screeching trucks sternly out of the station and onto the line.

The trucks tried very hard to make James give up, but he still kept on. Sometimes their brakes would slip on, and sometimes their axles would run hot. Each time the trouble had to be put right, and each time, James would start again. But he was not going to let them beat him.

"Give up! Give up! You can't pull us," shouted the trucks.

But James puffed on, and slowly he pulled them along the line. At last they saw Gordon's hill. This was the famous place where Gordon, the big proud engine, had once got stuck! Little Edward, one of the Tender Engines, had had to push Gordon up the hill!

As James came nearer to the hill, his driver warned him to be careful and to look out for trouble from the trucks.

"We'll go fast and get them up the hill before they know it," the driver whispered to James. "Don't let them stop you."

So James went faster and faster and soon they were half-way up the hill.

"I'm doing it! I'm doing it!" he panted. "Will the top ever come?"

Then with a sudden jerk, it all became much easier. James thought it was over and that he had pulled the trucks to the top of the hill without any trouble. But his driver shut off steam.

"They've done it again," he said. "We've left our tail behind. Look!"

The last trucks were running backwards down the hill. The coupling had broken. But the guard stopped the trucks and climbed out to warn other engines.

"That's why it was so easy," said James, as he backed the other trucks carefully down the hill. "What silly things trucks are. There might have been an accident."

Edward had come along. He offered to help, but James had decided that *he* was going to pull these trucks by himself.

"Good," said Edward. "Don't let them beat you!"

James struggled slowly up the hill. He pulled and puffed as hard as he could. After a long time he finally pulled the trucks to the top.

"I've done it! I've done it!" he cried, and his driver cheered.

They reached the station safely and James was resting in the yard when Edward pulled up.

"Peep, peep!" he whistled.

Then James saw the Fat Controller. He thought that he would be in trouble. But the Fat Controller was smiling. He had been in Edward's train and he had seen everything.

"You've made the most troublesome trucks on the line behave," he said. "After that, you deserve to keep your red coat!"

Gordon Off the Rails

Gordon was resting in a siding. Sometimes, when he was resting, he would say to himself, "It's really *very* tiring to be such a large and splendid engine. One does have to keep up appearances so."

At that moment Henry came by. "Peep, peep! Peep, peep! Hello, Fatface!" whistled Henry. Gordon had not seen Henry for some time.

"What a cheek!" he spluttered. "That Henry is getting too big for his wheels. Fancy speaking to me like that! *Meeee*!" he went on, letting off steam. "*Meee* who has never had an accident!"

Percy heard Gordon's last remark and he knew that it wasn't true.

"Aren't burst safety valves accidents?" Percy asked, innocently.

Gordon was very cross. He didn't like being teased and he knew that Percy was talking about the time when he, Gordon, had pulled the express too fast and had burst a safety valve.

"No indeed! High spirits! Might happen to any engine!" replied Gordon, huffily. "But, to come off the rails like Henry did when he was pulling *The Flying Kipper* . . . well, I ask you!" he went on. "Is it right? Is it decent?"

A few days later it was Henry's turn to take the express. Gordon watched him getting ready.

"Be careful, Henry," he said. "You're not pulling *The Flying Kipper* now! Mind you keep on the rails today!"

Henry snorted away. Gordon yawned and went to sleep.

But he didn't sleep for very long.

"Wake up, Gordon!" said his driver. "A special train is coming in and we're to pull it."

"Is it coaches or trucks?" asked Gordon, sleepily.

"Trucks," said his driver.

"Trucks!" said Gordon, crossly. "Pah!"

The men lit Gordon's fire and oiled him ready for the run. He needed to go on the turntable first so that he would be facing the right way. His fire was slow to start and wouldn't burn. They couldn't wait so Edward was called to help Gordon to the turntable.

"I won't go. I won't go," grumbled Gordon.

"Don't be silly. Don't be silly," puffed Edward.

At last Gordon was on the turntable. Edward was uncoupled and he backed away. Gordon's driver and fireman jumped down to turn him round. The movement had shaken Gordon's fire so that it was soon burning nicely.

Gordon was cross and he didn't care what he did. He waited until the table was halfway round and then his chance came. "I'll show them! I'll show them!" he hissed.

He moved slowly forward. He only meant to go a little way – just far enough to "jam" the turntable and stop it turning. But his plan was going wrong – he couldn't stop himself . . .

He slithered and slipped off the rails, down the embankment and settled in a ditch.

"OOOOOsh!" he hissed. "Get me out! Get me out!" he called.

His driver and fireman came to see him.

"Not a hope," said his driver. "You're stuck, you silly great engine, don't you understand that?"

They telephoned the Fat Controller. He could see Gordon from his window.

"So, Gordon didn't want to take the special train of trucks and ran into a ditch?" he answered from his office.

"What's that you say?" he went on. "The special's waiting – well, tell Edward to take it, please. And Gordon? Oh, leave him where he is. We haven't time to bother with him now!"

So there was Gordon, stuck in the ditch. Over on the other side, some little boys were chattering. "Coo!" they called. "Doesn't he look silly! They'll never get him out."

Then the boys began to sing:
Silly old Gordon fell in a ditch,
fell in a ditch,
fell in a ditch.
Silly old Gordon fell in a ditch,
all on a Monday morning!

Gordon lay in the ditch all day.

"Oh dear!" he thought. "I shall never get out."

But that evening the men brought floodlights. They used powerful jacks to lift Gordon and made a road of sleepers under his wheels to keep him out of the mud. Strong wire ropes were fastened to his back end and James and Henry, pulling hard, at last managed to bring Gordon back to the rails.

Late that night Gordon crawled home, a sadder and wiser engine.

Thomas Down the Mine

One day Thomas was at the junction when Gordon shuffled in with some trucks.

"Poof!" said Thomas. "What a funny smell! Can you smell a smell?"

"I can't smell a smell," said Annie.

"It's a funny, musty sort of smell," said Thomas.

"No one noticed it until you did," grunted Gordon. "It must be yours!" Not long ago Gordon had fallen into a dirty ditch. He knew that Thomas was teasing him about it.

"Annie and Clarabel, do you know what *I* think it is?" said Thomas. "It's ditchwater!" Gordon didn't have time to answer as Thomas was soon coupled to Annie and Clarabel and then he puffed quickly away.

Annie and Clarabel could hardly believe their ears. "He's *dreadfully* rude, I feel quite ashamed, I feel *quite* ashamed, he's dreadfully rude!" they twittered to each other.

They had great respect for Gordon, the big engine. "You mustn't be rude, you make us ashamed," they kept telling Thomas. But Thomas didn't care a bit.

"That was funny, that was funny," he chuckled, feeling very pleased with himself.

Thomas left the coaches at the station and went off to a mine for some trucks. Long ago, miners digging for lead had made tunnels under the ground. The tunnel roofs were strong enough to hold trucks, but they could not take the weight of the heavy engines. A large notice said: "DANGER. ENGINES MUST NOT PASS THIS POINT."

Thomas had been warned but he didn't care. He had often tried to pass the sign before but had never succeeded. He knew the rules; he had to push empty trucks into one siding and wait to collect full ones from another.

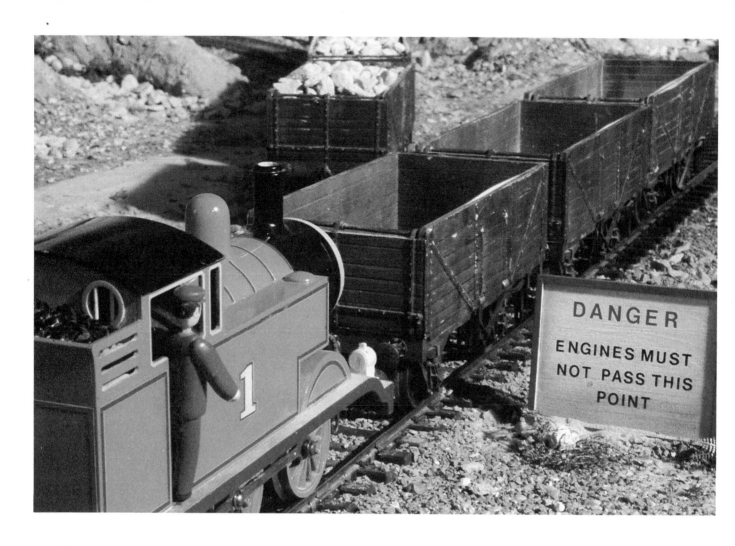

This morning he laughed as he puffed along. He had made a plan. "Silly old board!" he said to himself, getting nearer and nearer to the danger sign. The driver stopped him and the fireman went to turn the points. "Now for my plan," said Thomas and he bumped the trucks fiercely, jerking the driver off the footplate!

"Hurrah!" said Thomas, as he followed the trucks into a siding.

"Come back!" called his driver. But it was too late.

"Stupid old board!" said Thomas, as he ran past it. "There's no danger! There's no danger!"

"Look out!" cried the driver. The fireman clambered into the cab and tried Thomas's brakes.

There was a rumbling noise and the rails quivered. The fireman jumped clear. Then the rails sagged and broke.

"Fire and smoke!" said Thomas. "I'm sunk!" – and he was! Thomas could just see out of the hole but he couldn't move. "Oh dear!" he said. "I *am* a silly engine."

"And a very naughty one, too," said the Fat Controller, who had just arrived. "I saw you."

"Please get me out. I won't be naughty again," said Thomas.

"I'm not sure," said the Fat Controller. "We can't lift you out with a crane because the ground is not firm enough. Hmm . . . let me see . . . I wonder if Gordon could pull you out."

"Yes, sir," said Thomas, nervously. He didn't want to see Gordon just yet.

When Gordon heard about Thomas he laughed very loudly. "Down a mine is he? Ho! Ho! Ho! What a joke! What a joke!" he chortled, puffing quickly to the rescue. "Poop! Poop! Little Thomas," Gordon whistled. "We'll have you out in a couple of puffs. Poop! Poop! Poop!"

The men fastened strong cables between Gordon and Thomas.

"Are you ready? HEAVE!" called the Fat Controller.

But they didn't pull Thomas out in two puffs. It was a lot harder than they had all thought. Gordon worked hard but it took a long time to finally pull Thomas out of the hole.

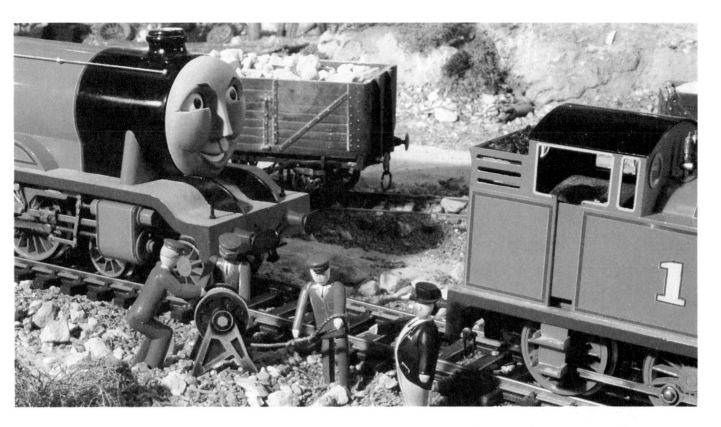

"I'm sorry I was cheeky," said Thomas.

"That's all right, Thomas," said Gordon. "You made me laugh!"

Thomas was very pleased that Gordon was not angry with him any more.

Thomas's fire had gone out so he needed a pull back to the station. "Can we go together?" asked Thomas.

"Of course we can," said Gordon. "I'll pull you back."

"Thank you very much," said Thomas. And buffer to buffer the two friends puffed home.

Thomas and Bertie

One day Thomas was waiting at a junction when a bus came into the yard.

"Hullo!" said Thomas. "Who are you?"

"I'm Bertie," said the bus. "Who are you?"

"I'm Thomas. I run this branch line."

Bertie laughed. "Ah – I remember now!" he said. "You were stuck in the snow. I had to take your passengers, then Terence the tractor had to pull you out! I've come to help you with your passengers today."

"Help *me*?" said Thomas, crossly. "I can go faster than you," he said, going bluer than ever and letting off steam.

"You can't," said Bertie.

"I can," huffed Thomas.

"I'll race you!" said Bertie.

Their drivers agreed to the race. The Station Master shouted, "Are you ready? GO!" – and they were off!

It always took Thomas a little while to build up speed so Bertie quickly drew in front.

Thomas was running well but he did not hurry. "Why don't you go fast? Why don't you go fast?" called Annie and Clarabel, who were running along behind.

"Wait and see. Wait and see," hissed Thomas.

"He's a long way ahead, a long way ahead," they cried, anxiously.

But Thomas didn't mind; he had remembered the level crossing.

There was Bertie fuming at the crossing gates while they sailed gaily through.

"Goodbye, Bertie!" called Thomas.

After that the road left the railway and went through a village. They couldn't see Bertie any more.

Before long they had to stop at a station to let off passengers. "Peep, pip, peep! Quickly, please," called Thomas. Everybody got out quickly. The guard blew his whistle and off they went again.

"Come along! Come along!" sang Thomas.

"We're coming along! We're coming along!" said Annie and Clarabel.

Thomas looked straight ahead and whistled in horror. There was Bertie crossing the bridge over the railway, tooting triumphantly on his horn!

"Oh, deary me! Oh, deary me!" groaned Thomas.

"Steady, Thomas," said Thomas's driver. "We'll beat Bertie yet."

Annie and Clarabel joined in. "We'll beat Bertie yet! We'll beat Bertie yet!" they sang.

"We'll do it! We'll do it!" puffed Thomas, bravely. "Oh bother, there's a station."

As Thomas stopped at the station he heard Bertie, tooting loudly.

"Goodbye, Thomas! You must be tired," called Bertie, as he raced by. "Sorry I can't stop; we *buses* have to work you know! Goodbye."

"Oh, dear!" thought Thomas. "We've lost." But he felt better after a drink. Then the signal dropped to show that the line was clear and they were off again.

As they rumbled over the bridge they saw Bertie waiting at the traffic lights. When the lights turned green, Bertie started with a roar and chased on after Thomas again. Road and railway ran up the valley side by side. By now Thomas had reached his full speed. Bertie tried hard but Thomas was too fast.

On and on they raced. Excited passengers cheered and shouted across the valley as Thomas whistled triumphantly and plunged into the tunnel, leaving Bertie toiling far behind.

"We've done it! We've done it!" chanted Annie and Clarabel happily, as they whooshed into the last station.

Everybody was there to give Thomas three cheers for winning the race. They all gave Bertie a big welcome too.

"Well done, Thomas!" said Bertie. "That was fun. But to beat you over that hill I should have had to grow wings and be an aeroplane!"

Now Thomas and Bertie keep each other very busy. Bertie finds people in the villages who want to go by train and takes them to Thomas, while Thomas brings people to the station for Bertie to take home.

Bertie and Thomas often talk about their race. But Bertie's passengers don't like being bounced like peas in a frying pan! The Fat Controller has warned Thomas not to race at dangerous speeds. So although Thomas and Bertie would like to have another race, I don't think they ever will. Do you?

Thomas and the Trucks

Thomas the Tank Engine wouldn't stop being a nuisance. Night after night he kept the other engines awake.

"I'm tired of pushing coaches. I want to see the world."

The other engines didn't take much notice, for Thomas was a little engine with a long tongue.

But one night, Edward came to the shed. He was a kind little engine, and felt sorry for Thomas.

"I've got some trucks to take home tomorrow. If you take them instead of me I'll push coaches in the yard."

"Thank you," said Thomas, "that will be nice."

Next morning Edward and Thomas asked their drivers, and when they said "Yes," Thomas ran off happily to find the trucks. Now trucks are silly and noisy. They talk a lot and don't attend to what they are doing. And I'm sorry to say, they play tricks on an engine who is not used to them.

Edward knew all about trucks. He warned Thomas to be careful, but Thomas was too excited to listen. The shunter fastened the coupling, and when the signal dropped Thomas was ready. The guard blew his whistle.

"Peep! Peep!" answered Thomas and started off.

But the trucks weren't ready.

"Oh, oh, oh," they screamed. "Wait Thomas, wait."

But Thomas wouldn't wait. "Come on, come on," he puffed.

"All right, all right, don't fuss, all right, don't fuss," grumbled the trucks.

Thomas began going faster and faster.

"Wheeeee," he whistled, as he rushed through Henry's tunnel.

Then he was out into the open countryside once more.

They rumbled past fields and they clattered through stations.

"Hurry, hurry," called Thomas. He was feeling very proud of himself. But the trucks grew crosser and crosser. At last Thomas slowed down as he came to Gordon's hill.

"Steady now, steady," warned the driver, as they reached the top.

He began to put on the brakes.

"We're stopping, we're stopping," called Thomas.

"No, no, no, no!" answered the trucks, bumping into each other. "Go on, go on."

Before the driver could stop them, they had pushed Thomas down the hill and were rattling and laughing behind him. Poor Thomas tried hard to stop them from making him go too fast.

"Stop pushing, stop pushing," he hissed, but the trucks took no notice.

"Go on, go on," they giggled in their silly way.

Thomas was travelling much too fast and at any moment he would reach the next station.

"There's the station. Oh dear, what shall I do?" he cried.

They rattled straight through and swerved into the goods yard.

Thomas shut his eyes. "I must stop."

When he opened his eyes he saw he had stopped just in front of the buffers.

There watching him was the Fat Controller.

"What are you doing here, Thomas?" he asked.

"I've brought Edward's trucks," Thomas answered.

"Why did you come so fast?"

"I didn't mean to. I was pushed," said Thomas.

"You've got a lot to learn about trucks then, little Thomas. After pushing them about here for a few weeks you'll know almost as much about them as Edward does. Then you'll be a Really Useful Engine."

Stories first published 1990 by Buzz Books
an imprint of Reed Children's Books
Michelin House, 81 Fulham Road, London SW3 6RB
and Auckland, Melbourne, Singapore and Toronto
This edition published 1992 by Dean
in association with Heinemann Young Books
Copyright © William Heinemann Ltd 1990
Reprinted 1992 (twice), 1993 (three times), 1994 (twice)
All publishing rights; William Heinemann Ltd
All television and merchandising rights licensed by
William Heinemann Ltd to Britt Allcroft (Thomas) Ltd
exclusively, worldwide
Photographs © Britt Allcroft (Thomas) Ltd 1985, 1986
Photographs by David Mitton, Kenny McArthur and
Terry Permane for Britt Allcroft's production of
Thomas the Tank Engine and Friends
Produced by Mandarin Offset
Printed in China
ISBN 0 603 55045 2
A CIP catalogue record for this book is available in the British Library